A Busy Day
at the
Garage

PHILIPPE DUPASQUIER

CANDLEWICK PRESS
CAMBRIDGE, MASSACHUSETTS

Early in the morning, on the way to work,
something goes wrong with John Walker's car.
He leaves it outside the garage.

The garage is not open yet.

Mr. Fingers arrives, with Mick and Mack, the mechanics, and Pete, the gas pump attendant.

Pete tries to start Mr. Walker's car, but it
won't go. "Push it, boys!" Mr. Fingers says.
Beryl, the cashier, opens up the sales booth.

The car transporter arrives with new cars
for Mr. Fingers to sell.

Mick and Mack start to work on Mr. Walker's car.

Pete serves his first customer.

"My mom would like that sports car," Jimmy says
to his school friends.
"Slowly now!" says Mr. Fingers.

"This car is a real wreck," Mick says.

"Here's your change," Beryl says to the customer, who counts out the money.

Graham Slick puts air in his tires.

The gasoline tanker delivers gasoline.

Everyone is hard at work, which makes
Mr. Fingers happy.

Graham's girlfriend, Molly, opens her umbrella,
but it blows inside out.

"What a downpour!" Mack says.

"It's just a passing shower," says Beryl.

The tow truck brings in a smashed car.

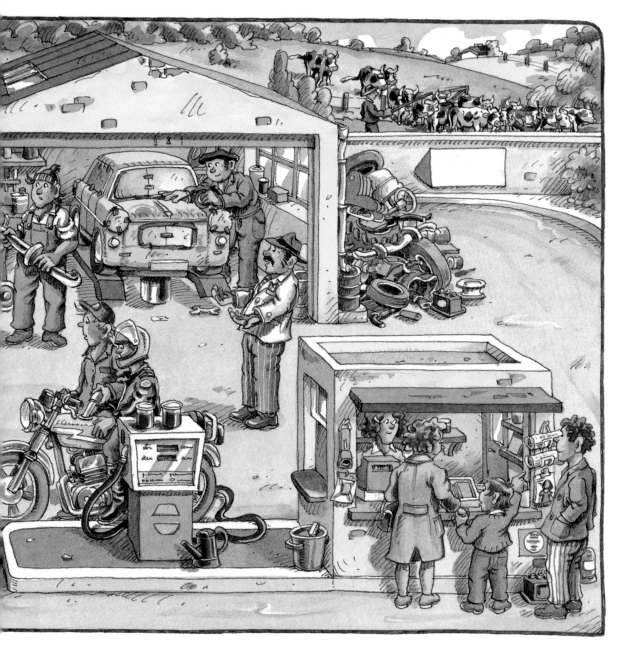

"Straight ahead!" says Mr. Fingers.

"Here comes another one!" Mick says.

"Whoops!" says George. "Look at my tire!"
But everyone is looking at the smashed car.

"I skidded right off the road," the driver tells Mick.

Mr. Walker comes to pick up his car.

Beryl locks up the booth.

Mr. Walker drives away, very pleased that his
car has been fixed.

Mick gives Mack a lift home on his motorcycle.

Mr. Fingers is the last to leave.

Whoops, Mr. Fingers, what a way to end
a busy day!

IF THIS BOOK IS ONE OF YOUR CHILD'S FAVORITES, WHY NOT BUY
ANOTHER COPY TO PUT SAFELY ASIDE AS A KEEPSAKE?
YOUR CHILD AND YOUR CHILD'S CHILDREN WILL THANK YOU!

PHILIPPE DUPASQUIER studied illustration and advertising in France.
While in college, he spent three months in England, and was so impressed
by the quality of illustration there that he decided to move there. He says
his style was influenced in part by his long fascination with comics.
"[They] have always been important to me, and in France they are are a
recognized form of illustration." Philippe Dupasquier is the author of
many books for children, including the award-winning *Dear Daddy*.